Story play™

This book belongs to

_____.

This book was read by

_____

on

_____.

Are you ready to start reading the **StoryPlay** way?

Read the story on its own. Play the activities together
as you read!

Ready. Set. Smart!

To Dianne Hess, with love!
~ J.A.

To Larson, Dianne, and David
~ B.M.

Scholastic Inc., 557 Broadway, New York, NY 10012
Scholastic UK Ltd., Euston House, 24 Eversholt Street, London NW1 1DB United Kingdom

Library of Congress Cataloging-in-Publication Data available • ISBN 978-1-338-18734-2
10 9 8 7 6 5 4 3 2 1   17 18 19 20 21 • Printed in Panyu, China   137
This edition first printing, October 2017 • Book design by Doan Buu

The Gingerbread Man

retold by Jim Aylesworth
illustrated by Barbara McClintock

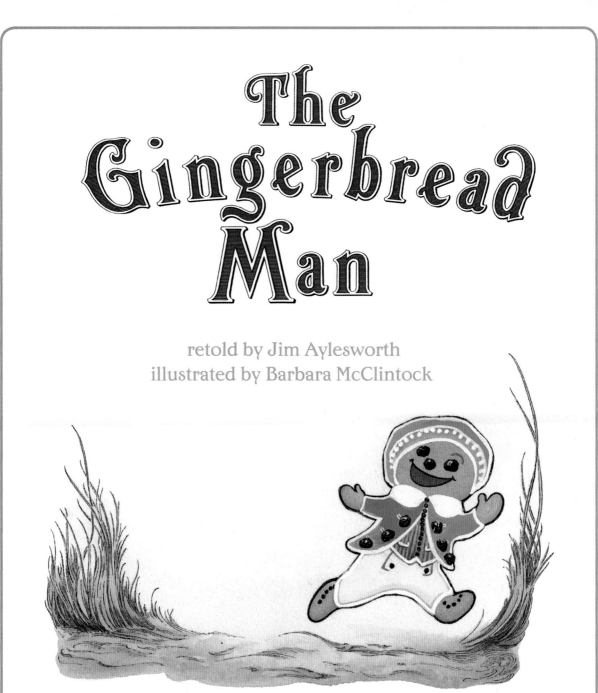

CARTWHEEL BOOKS • AN IMPRINT OF SCHOLASTIC INC.

Once upon a time,

there was a little old man and a little old woman.

One day, the little old woman said,
"Let's make a gingerbread man!"
"Yes, let's do!" said the little old man, and they did.

So, they mixed
up the batter,

and they rolled
out the dough,

and they shaped
the little arms,

and they shaped
the little legs,

and they shaped
the little head.

And with raisins, they made the little eyes and the little nose and the little mouth, and then with sugar glaze, they dressed him in a fancy suit of clothes.

What do you think the little old man and woman are going to do with the gingerbread man next?

When all was set, they put the gingerbread man into the oven, and they waited.

How can you tell the gingerbread man is ready?

Pretty soon, the gingerbread man was ready, and so were they!

Why is the gingerbread man running away? Would you run away, too?

But when they opened the oven door,
out popped the Gingerbread Man,
and he ran across the floor.

The little old man and the little old woman could hardly believe their eyes! The Gingerbread Man looked up at them, put his little hands on his hips, and said,

"Run! Run!
Fast as you can!
You can't catch me!
I'm the Gingerbread Man!"

The little old man reached down to grab him, but quick as a wink, the Gingerbread Man ran out the door and down the road, and the little old man and the little old woman ran after him.

The words *CAN* and *MAN* rhyme. What other words rhyme with them?

"**Come back! Come back!**" yelled the little old man.
But the Gingerbread Man just looked over his shoulder,
and said,

"**No! No!
I won't come back!
I'd rather run
Than be your snack!**"

And he kept on running.

And he ran,

and he ran,

and he ran . . .

. . . and after a time, he met a butcher standing in front of his shop. The Gingerbread Man put his little hands on his hips, and said,

"Run! Run!
Fast as you can!
You can't catch me!
I'm the Gingerbread Man!
I've run from a husband!
I've run from a wife!
And I'll run from you, too!
I can! I can!"

What kind of food does a butcher sell?
How do you know?

The butcher reached down to grab him, but quick as a wink, the Gingerbread Man ran on down the road, and the butcher ran after him!

"Come back!" yelled the butcher.

And not far behind, the little old man and the little old woman were yelling, too! **"Come back! Come back!"**

But the Gingerbread Man just looked over his shoulder, and said,

"No! No!
I won't come back!
I'd rather run
Than be your snack!"

And he kept on running! And he ran, and he ran, and he ran.

And after a time, he met a black-and-white cow. The Gingerbread Man looked up at her, put his little hands on his hips, and said,

"Run! Run!
Fast as you can!
You can't catch me!
I'm the Gingerbread Man!
I've run from a husband!
I've run from a wife!
I've run from a butcher
With a carving knife!
And I'll run from you, too!
I can! I can!"

The black-and-white cow reached out to grab him. But quick as a wink, the Gingerbread Man ran on down the road, and the black-and-white cow ran after him!

"Come back!" yelled the black-and-white cow.

And not far behind, the little old man, and the little old woman, and the butcher with the knife were yelling, too!

"Come back! Come back! Come back!"

But the Gingerbread Man just looked over his shoulder, and said,

"No! No!
I won't come back!
I'd rather run
Than be your snack!"

And he kept on running. And he ran, and he ran, and he ran.

How many characters are chasing the gingerbread man now?

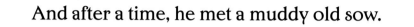

And after a time, he met a muddy old sow.

The Gingerbread Man looked up at her,
put his little hands on his hips, and said,

"Run! Run!
Fast as you can!
You can't catch me!
I'm the Gingerbread Man!
I've run from a husband!
I've run from a wife!
I've run from a butcher
With a carving knife!
I've run from a cow
All black and white!
And I'll run from you, too!
I can! I can!"

The muddy old sow reached out to grab him. But quick as a wink, the Gingerbread Man ran on down the road, and the muddy old sow ran after him!

"**Come back!**" yelled the muddy old sow.

And not far behind, the little old man, and the little old woman, and the butcher with the knife, and the black-and-white cow were yelling, too!

"**Come back! Come back! Come back! Come back!**"

Do you think anyone will catch the gingerbread man?

But the Gingerbread Man just looked over his shoulder, and said,

**"No! No!
I won't come back!
I'd rather run
Than be your snack!"**

And he kept on running.

And he ran,

and he ran,

and he ran.

Do you remember the order in which the characters chased the gingerbread man?

And after a time, he met a fox. The Gingerbread Man looked at him, put his little hands on his hips, and said,

"Run! Run!
Fast as you can!
You can't catch me!
I'm the Gingerbread Man!
I've run from a husband!
I've run from a wife!
I've run from a butcher
With a carving knife!
I've run from a cow
And a muddy old sow,
And I'll run from you, too!
I can! I can!"

"What did you say?" asked the fox. The tricky fox pretended that he couldn't hear well. "I'm not as young as I used to be," he said. "You'll have to come closer and speak louder."

The Gingerbread Man stepped closer, and in a very loud voice, he said,

"Run! Run!
Fast as you can!
You can't catch me!
I'm the Gingerbread Man!
I've run from a husband!
I've run from a wife!
I've run from a butcher
With a carving knife!
I've run from a cow,
And a muddy old sow!
And I'll run from you, too!
I can! I can!"

Just then, the little old man, and the little old woman, and the butcher with the knife, and the black-and-white cow, and the muddy old sow came running around a turn in the road! And they were yelling! **"Come back! Come back! Come back! Come back! Come back!"**

The Gingerbread Man looked over
his shoulder, but before he could
say a single word, the fox jumped up
and grabbed him!

And quick as a wink,
Before he could think,
The Gingerbread Man
Was gone!

The little old man, and the little old woman, and the butcher with the knife, and the black-and-white cow, and the muddy old sow all stood and stared sadly at the fox. He hadn't left a single crumb for anyone.

Riddle-riddle ran,
Fiddle-fiddle fan,
So ends the tale of
The Gingerbread Man.

How are the rest of the
characters feeling right now?

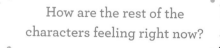

Story time fun never ends with these creative activities!

★ Search-and-Find Adventure! ★

While the gingerbread man goes on his own adventure, you can go on a search-and-find adventure! See if you can locate all of the items listed below somewhere in the book. Can you find at least:

one house

two horns

three paint brushes

four aprons

five firewood logs

six trees

seven buttons

eight legs

nine sausages

ten raisins

★ Write Your Own Ending! ★

In this story of the gingerbread man, the fox EATS the gingerbread man! If you were writing your own story about the gingerbread man, what would your ending be? Would the gingerbread man get away? Would he trick the fox? Make up your very own ending, and ask an adult to help you write it down. Happy storytelling!

★ Gingerbread Picture Time ★

The little old man and woman in the story created their very own gingerbread man, and now you can, too! Draw a picture of what your gingerbread man or woman would look like. You can decorate it any way you choose! Remember to sign your name!